Mommies Are Amazing

For Olly, Tommy, and Benji
—M.C.

To Ema and Mima, with love
—P.L.

Henry Holt and Company, LLC
Publishers since 1866
175 Fifth Avenue
New York, New York 10010
mackids.com

Library of Congress Cataloging-in-Publication Data is available.
ISBN 978-1-62779-651-4

Our books may be purchased in bulk for promotional, educational, or business use.
Please contact your local bookseller or the Macmillan Corporate and Premium Sales Department
at (800) 221-7945 ext. 5442 or by e-mail at MacmillanSpecialMarkets@macmillan.com.

First published in Australia in 2016 by Koala Books
First U.S. Edition—2017
Printed in China by Toppan Leefung Printing Ltd., Dongguan City, Guangdong Province

1 3 5 7 9 10 8 6 4 2

Mommies Are
Amazing

Meredith Costain

illustrated by **Polona Lovšin**

Henry Holt and Company
New York

Mommies are magic.

They kiss away troubles . . .

... find gold in the sunlight

and rainbows in bubbles.

Mommies are joyful,
the best of all friends.

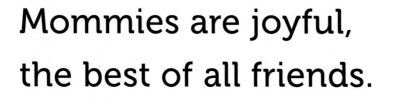

When playing together,
the fun never ends!

Mommies are fearless.
If you have a scare . . .

. . . they'll stay close beside you to show you they care.

Mommies are clever.
They know when you're sad.

They'll hug you and kiss you
when you're feeling bad.

Mommies are sporty.

They climb
and they leap.

They run and they tumble,

then curl up and sleep.

Mommies are tender.
They'll give you a hug . . .

. . . then tuck you in tightly,
so you're warm and snug.

My mommy's so special.

I tell her each day . . .

. . . just how much I love her

in every way!

May 2017

Dear Ashley,

Happy First Mother's Day!

Motherhood has a unique way of changing a woman to realize a commitment and priority to forever love, nurture and cherish her child. You're an extraordinary Mother and I love the way you love your child and embrace this new role amongst all others. You make me proud.

 Much Love,
  Mom